Steck-Vaughn

BRIDGES

TO

READING COMPREHENSION

Level C

STECK-VAUGHN

COMPANY

ELEMENTARY · SECONDARY · ADULT · LIBRARY

ACKNOWLEDGMENTS

EXECUTIVE EDITOR: Diane Sharpe

PROJECT EDITOR: Anne Souby

DESIGN MANAGER: Donna Brawley

PHOTO EDITOR: Margie Foster

PRODUCT DEVELOPMENT: Curriculum Concepts

ILLUSTRATION CREDITS: Unit 1 Steve Stankiewicz: pp.36, 42-43; Unit 2 Howard Berelson: pp.46-53, 55-61, 63-64; Toby Gowing: pp.66-73, 76-83; Unit 3 Laura Kelly: pp.109-115, 117-127.

PHOTO CREDITS: Unit 1 p.4 © United States Geological Survey; p.6 © Sue Ogrocki/Reuters/Bettmann; p.7 © Jeff Christensen/Gamma Liaison; p.8 © Ira Schwartz/Reuters/Bettmann; p.9 © M. Springer/ Gamma Liaison; p.10 © Gregory Foster/Gamma Liaison; p.11 © Jeff Christensen/Gamma Liaison; p.12 © Gregory Foster/Gamma Liaison; p.13 © M. Springer/Gamma Liaison; p.14 © Ira Schwartz/ Reuters/Bettmann; p.15 © Sue Ogrocki/Reuters/Bettmann; p.16 © Billy E. Barnes/Tony Stone Images; p.17 © David Petty/Photo Researchers; pp.18-19 © UPI/Bettmann; p.20 © David Petty/Photo Researchers; pp.21-22 © UPI/Bettmann; p.24 © Billy E. Barnes/Tony Stone Images; pp.25, 30 © Reuters/Bettmann; p.27 © Associated Press; p.28 © David Hardy/Science Photo Library; p.29 © Associated Press; p.35 © Jonathan Blair/Woodfin Camp; p.37 © Culver Pictures; p.38 © Ray Pfortner/Peter Arnold, Inc.; p.39 © Jonathan Blair/Woodfin Camp; p.40 © Culver Pictures; p.41 © Ray Pfortner/Peter Arnold, Inc.; Unit 2 p.44 (graduate) August Gabriel/Photo Researchers, (runner) Mark J. Goebel/Omni-Photo Communications; p.65 © Library of Congress; p.75 © Culver Pictures; p.85 © Library of Congress; Unit 3 p.86 © Gay Bumgarner/Tony Stone Images; p.88 © Christian Bossu-Pica/Tony Stone Images; p.89 © Animals Animals; p.90 © USDA Soil Conservation Service; p.91 © Library of Congress; p.92 © George Goodwin/Monkmeyer Press Photo Service; p.93 © USDA Soil Conservation Service; p.94 © Library of Congress; p.95 © Gay Bumgarner/ Tony Stone Images; p.96 © Animals Animals; p.97 © Christian Bossu-Pica/Tony Stone Images; p.98 © David Woodfall/Tony Stone Images; p.99 © Michael Dywer/Stock Boston; p.100 © Spencer Grant/Photo Research; p.101 © EPA; p.102 © Tony Freeman/PhotoEdit; p.103 © Richard Hutchings/ PhotoEdit; p.104 © Michael Dywer/Stock Boston; p.105 © Spencer Grant/Photo Research; p.106 © EPA; p.107 © Richard Hutchings/PhotoEdit.

Grateful acknowledgment is made for permission to reprint copyrighted material as follows:

Earthquakes by Keith Lye. Copyright © 1993 by Steck-Vaughn Company.

¡Viva Mexico! A Story of Benito Juárez and Cinco de Mayo by Argentina Palacios. Copyright © 1993 by Dialogue Systems, Inc.

Going West by Jean Van Leeuwen. Copyright © 1992 by Jean Van Leeuwen. Used by permission of Dial Books for Young Readers, a division of Penguin Books USA Inc.

Pollution by Herta S. Breiter. Copyright © 1991 by Steck-Vaughn Company.

And Still the Turtle Watched by Sheila MacGill-Callahan. Copyright © 1991 by Sheila MacGill-Callahan, text. Used by permission of Dial Books for Young Readers, a division of Penguin Books USA Inc.

CONTENTS

1 NATURAL DISASTERS

What is a natural disaster?

A natural disaster is what happens when nature causes damage. A big storm such as a hurricane can be a natural disaster. Other examples of natural disasters are floods, earthquakes, and volcanoes. Most natural disasters happen suddenly. They can wreck homes and property. Sometimes people are hurt, too. You will learn more about natural disasters as you read this unit.

What Do You Already Know?

Think about natural disasters that you have seen on television or in the movies. Or, think of a time you were in a big storm. Write a paragraph that tells about what you saw and how you felt.

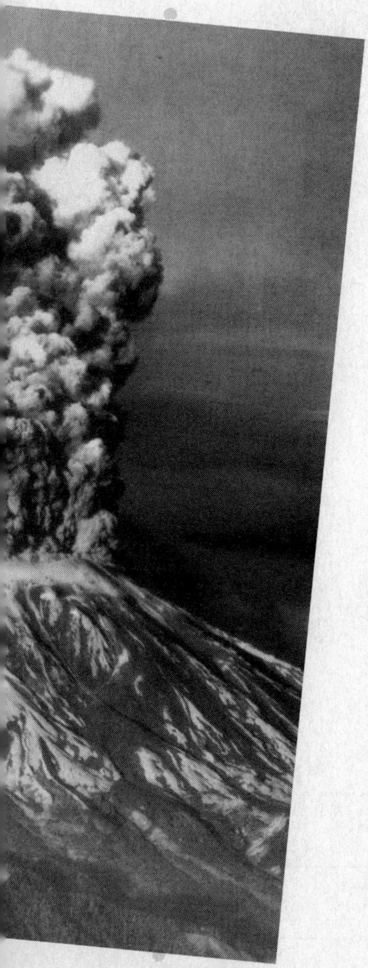

_____

_____

_____

_____

_____

_____

_____

What Do You Want to Find Out?

You will find out many things about natural disasters in this unit. What would you like to learn about natural disasters? On the lines below, write some questions you want answered. You may find the answers to your questions as you read.

_____

_____

_____

_____

_____

_____

GETTING READY TO READ

The first story you will read is "Flood!" Can you imagine being in a giant flood? If you had time, what would you do to get ready for a flood?

What Do You Think You Will Learn?

Look through "Flood!" on pages 7–10. What do the pictures show? What do you think you will learn when you read this story? Write your ideas below.

_____

_____

_____

_____

_____

Flood!

What Is a Flood?

Sometimes spring rains are good news. After a cold, dry winter, plants and trees need rainwater. But too much rain can mean trouble. During a storm, rainwater goes into the ground. It also goes into streams and rivers. But the earth can only hold so much water.

Too much rain can cause streams, rivers, and lakes to spill over onto the land. This is a flood. During a bad flood, a river of water can race through a town. The water can fill up yards and houses. It can carry off cars, houses, and people.

Flood waters can reach the tops of houses and cover their roofs.

Where Do Floods Happen?

Big rainstorms have caused flooding in many parts of the world. Land by the ocean or near a river is usually the first to flood. A sea storm may cause flooding near the ocean. Rain and wind can make the flooding worse. Homes by the shore are sometimes washed away.

After days or weeks of rain, rivers become full of water. The water can spill over onto the land around it. It can flood cities and farms. Big floods do not happen very often. When they do happen, they can wash away homes. They can ruin stores. They can wreck farms and cause damage to crops.

The Mississippi River Floods

The Mississippi River is one of the world's largest rivers. It runs north and south through the middle of the United States. Millions of people live along the river.

In April 1993 heavy rains hit land along the Mississippi River. By August more than three feet of rain had fallen in some places. The river got bigger and bigger. People used sandbags to build walls along the riverbanks. They wanted to stop the river from flooding the farms and towns nearby.

Nothing could hold the river back. The walls fell down. The river rushed through city streets. It flooded homes. Farms were covered with water.

Floods in the United States have not been as bad as floods in China, India, and other countries. But the Mississippi River floods caused terrible damage. The flood damage cost ten billion dollars.

When the Mississippi River flooded streets and homes, people got around in boats.

Can People Stop Floods?

People cannot stop floods. There are some ways to hold back or control floods, but even these don't always work. One way is to plant grass and trees near rivers. The roots of plants drink in water from wet ground. This helps soak up extra water. Another way is to build walls made of dirt or sandbags along the riverbanks. These walls are called levees. They help keep the river from flooding onto the land nearby.

These men are using sandbags to build a wall, or levee, along the riverbank.

Dams can also control floods. These giant walls are made of concrete. They hold back water and store it to use later. On the ocean people build sea walls. Sea walls keep large waves from hitting the houses and the seashore.

Some people think the best way to control floods is to plan where to build. They think houses should not be built near places that flood. Levees and dams sometimes break. Sea walls wear down. At those times, towns and farms are in danger. If there were no buildings near places that flood, people wouldn't have to worry about finding their houses or barns under water.

AFTER READING

What Did You Learn?

You have read "Flood!" for the first time. Now look back at what you wrote on page 6. Did you learn what you thought you would learn? What was most interesting to you? Write two new things you learned below.

_____

_____

_____

Check Your Understanding

Darken the circle next to the word or words that best complete each sentence.

1. Floods happen when the earth cannot hold any more _____.

   Ⓐ trees   Ⓒ houses

   Ⓑ water   Ⓓ people

2. Very bad floods begin near _____ and oceans.

   Ⓐ cities   Ⓒ rivers

   Ⓑ towns   Ⓓ farmland

3. In 1993 the _____ floods cost billions of dollars.

   Ⓐ Missouri River   Ⓒ Snake River

   Ⓑ Mississippi River   Ⓓ Columbia River

4. Dirt or sandbag _____ can help control river floods.

   Ⓐ sea wall   Ⓒ dam

   Ⓑ houses   Ⓓ levees

Vocabulary — Compound Words

A compound word is made up of two smaller words. The two smaller words can often help you figure out the meaning of the compound word.

> **Walls made of sandbags or dirt can hold back water.**

Sandbags is made up of two smaller words, sand and bags. Think about what each word means. It will help you figure out that sandbags are bags filled with sand.

Find the compound word in each sentence below. Write the two smaller words on the lines. Then write the meaning of the compound word.

1. The raindrops made puddles of water on the ground.

_____   _____

_____

2. It rained from early afternoon until evening.

_____   _____

_____

3. People needed rowboats to get from place to place.

_____   _____

_____

4. The rainstorm caused heavy flood damage.

_____   _____

_____

Words That Were New to You

Choose some words from the story that were new to you. Use a dictionary to check the meanings. Add the words and their meanings to your word list on page 128.

REREADING

Main Idea and Details

A main idea is the most important idea in a paragraph. It tells what a paragraph is all about. Details tell the reader more about the main idea. Read this paragraph from "Flood!"

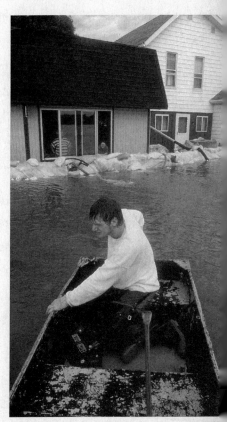

> Nothing could hold the river back. The walls fell down. The river rushed through city streets. It flooded homes. Farms were covered with water.

In this paragraph, the first sentence tells the main idea. But the main idea can be in other places, too. Sometimes two sentences tell the main idea. Other sentences in the paragraph give details about the main idea.

Reread "Flood!" As you read, look for sentences that tell what each paragraph is about. Then, look for details that tell more about the main idea.

After you reread "Flood!" write two details that tell more about each main idea below.

1. Main Idea: In April 1993 heavy rains hit land along the Mississippi River. (page 9)

   DETAIL:_____

   DETAIL:_____

2. Main Idea: There are some ways to hold back or control floods. (page 10)

   DETAIL:_____

   DETAIL:_____

STUDY SKILLS

Alphabetical Order

The alphabet has 26 letters. Each letter has a special place, or order, in the alphabet. This order is called alphabetical order.

The words below are listed in alphabetical order. The word that begins with the letter a comes first. The word that begins with the letter b comes second. The word that comes next begins with the letter r, because r comes after b and before s in the alphabet.

> after
> below
> river
> sea
> spill
> storm

There is more than one word in the list that begins with the letter s. When two or more words begin with the same letter, you must look at the second letter in each word.

> sea
> spill
> storm

The letter e comes before p in the alphabet. So, sea comes before spill. Storm comes after spill because the letter t comes after the letter p.

Read the words in the box. Go through the alphabet, and put the words in alphabetical order. If two words start with the same letter, look at the second letter. Write the words on the lines. Check them off the list as you go.

river	1. _____
ocean	2. _____
flood	3. _____
places	4. _____
people	5. _____

Check Yourself

Use a dictionary. Find the word listed just before ocean and the word listed just after ocean. What are the two words that you found?

THINK and WRITE

Use what you have learned to complete one of these activities.

1. Imagine that your farm near the Mississippi River flooded. Write a letter to a friend about it.

2. Write a speech to give at the town hall. Tell why you are for or against building a dam on a nearby river.

3. Write a poem called "Flood!" Draw a picture to go with your poem.

GETTING READY TO READ

You have read about floods. Were you surprised at the damage water can do? Water is not the only thing that can cause damage. Wind can, too!

What Do You Think You Will Learn?

Look through "Twister!" on pages 17–19. What natural disaster do you think it will tell about? What else do you think you will learn? Write your ideas below.

_____

_____

_____

_____

_____

_____

_____

Twister!

Picture this. Your family is sitting down to dinner. It has been hot and sticky all day. Suddenly, the air grows still. You look out the window. The sky is very dark. A giant black cloud races toward your home. The cloud is shaped like a giant funnel. It sucks up trees and houses. "It's a twister!" someone shouts. Twister is a nickname for a tornado.

Wind blows out the windows in your house. The walls begin to shake. Glass flies everywhere. Your family runs for cover down in the cellar. Soon you hear a terrible roar. It sounds like 1,000 trains are moving through the house. A tornado has hit.

It's over in a few minutes. When you go upstairs again, you can't believe the sight. The walls of your house have fallen over like cardboard. Outside, cars are crushed like paper cups. Some of the houses nearby are flat. Someone's roof has been lifted up by the wind. It sits in the middle of the street.

If you see a dark cloud shaped like a funnel nearby, get out of the way. It's a tornado!

The World's Most Dangerous Storms

Thousands of people have lived through tornadoes. They have seen their homes and towns ruined. More tornadoes hit the United States than any other country. Every year in the spring and summer about 850 tornadoes strike the U.S. Some cause no damage. Others wipe out whole towns.

Tornadoes are known for their fast, twisting winds. Inside a tornado, winds move at up to 500 miles per hour. These giant winds make tornadoes the most dangerous storms in the world. Scientists are not really sure how tornadoes begin. What they do know is nothing can be done to control them or stop them.

Sometimes tornadoes hit the same places over and over again. In 1974, 148 tornadoes hit five states in the U.S. In 1985, 41 tornadoes cut through the Ohio Valley and Canada. Five years later, 50 tornadoes crashed into the midwestern United States.

Tornadoes can wipe out some houses on a street and leave others standing.

After a tornado, neighbors work together to find people's things and clean up.

Help from Near and Far

What happened after the 1985 tornadoes shows how people get through disasters. These tornadoes killed 90 people. They ruined houses and farms. They scattered people's things everywhere.

People from many different places traveled to the Ohio Valley to help. They helped to clean up. Then, they helped to build the towns again. Gifts came in from all over the country. People sent food and clothes. Others sent money and medicine.

Neighbors reached out to help each other. Stores gave away food, clothing, wood, and nails. Doctors, nurses, and Red Cross workers helped. Young and old worked together day and night. Soon new houses, barns, and buildings went up. So much good will made people feel better.

One person said, "You don't realize how good people are until something like this happens. They can't do enough for you."

AFTER READING

What Did You Learn?

You have read "Twister!" for the first time. Now look back at what you wrote on page 16. Were you surprised by anything you learned? Tell what surprised you the most. Write your answers on the lines below.

_____

_____

_____

Check Your Understanding

Read each sentence. Look at the words and numbers in the box. Choose one to complete each sentence. Write each word or number on the correct line.

500	850	twister
minutes	dangerous	funnel

1. Another name for a tornado is _____.

2. Every year there are about _____ tornadoes in the U.S.

3. Inside a tornado, the winds may be as fast as

   _____ miles per hour.

4. Tornadoes last for only a few _____.

5. Tornadoes are the most _____ storms in the world.

6. A tornado cloud is shaped like a _____.

Vocabulary — Inflectional Endings

A verb is an action word. When you add -s or -es to a verb, the action happens in the present. When you add -ed to a verb, the action happened in the past. Read these sentences.

1. Now a neighbor helps to clean up.

2. He pushes broken glass out of the way now.

3. Many people helped after the tornado.

The words help and push are action words. In sentence 1, -s is added to help. Helps tells what the neighbor is doing now.

In sentence 2, -es is added to push. Pushes tells what the man is doing now.

In sentence 3, -ed is added to help. Helped tells what people did in the past.

Read the sentences below. Circle the word that best completes each sentence.

1. A tornado _____ the schools and buildings yesterday.

     wrecks   wrecked

2. Now people watch as the building _____ to the ground.

     crashed   crashes

3. Last year the tornado _____ cars around like toys.

     scatters   scattered

Words That Were New to You

Choose words from the story that were new to you. Use a dictionary to check the meanings. Add the words and their meanings to your word list on page 128.

REREADING

Compare and Contrast

You have read about tornadoes and floods. How are these disasters the same? How are they different? When you show how two things are alike and different, you compare and contrast. Read these sentences.

1. Floods and tornadoes are both natural disasters.

2. Floods happen when the earth cannot hold any more water.

3. Scientists are not really sure how tornadoes happen.

The first sentence tells how floods and tornadoes are alike. They are both natural disasters. Sentences 2 and 3 tell one way that floods and tornadoes are different. People know how floods happen. They don't know how tornadoes happen.

Look at the chart below. It gives some information about floods. Reread "Twister!" to find out how tornadoes and floods are the same and different. After you reread the story, finish the chart below.

	Floods	Tornadoes
1. Why do they happen?	the earth cannot hold any more water	no one is really sure
2. Can they be controlled?	yes	
3. Can they be stopped?	no	
4. When do they happen?	after a lot of rain	
5. What damage happens?	homes, buildings, and crops are destroyed	

Main Idea and Details

Write a detail from the story that tells more about each main idea below.

1. Main Idea: Sometimes tornadoes hit the same places over and over again. (page 18)

   DETAIL: _____

   _____

2. Main Idea: Neighbors reached out to help each other. (page 19)

   DETAIL: _____

   _____

STUDY SKILLS

Dictionary — Guide Words

Words in the dictionary are listed in alphabetical order. The first letter of a word tells you where to start looking. Guide words can also help you find a word. They tell you the first word and the last word on the page.

Is tornado on the same page as the guide words toothpick and toss? Here's how to find out.

> toothpick • toss
>
> **tooth·pick** [tōōth'pĭk'] *noun, plural* **toothpicks.** a small, thin piece of wood, plastic, or other material, used for removing food from between the teeth.
> **top¹** [tŏp] *noun, plural* **tops.** **1.** the highest part or point of something: The roof is the *top* of a building. **2.** the highest level or degree: He yells at the *top* of his voice.

T ▶ Look at the first letter.
   T is in both guide words. (**t**oothpick **t**oss)

O ▶ Look at the second letter.
   O is in both guide words. (t**o**othpick t**o**ss)

R ▶ Look at the third letter. (t**o**othpick to**s**s)
   R comes between O and S. (**o** p q **r s**)

Tornado would be on this dictionary page.

Darken the circle next to the word you would find on a dictionary page with these guide words.

1. flip - flood

   Ⓐ fire   Ⓒ fluffy

   Ⓑ flock   Ⓓ fleece

2. turtle - twister

   Ⓐ twin   Ⓒ trunk

   Ⓑ two   Ⓓ town

3. levee - life

   Ⓐ letter   Ⓒ lick

   Ⓑ leg   Ⓓ lily

Check Yourself

Look up hurricane in the dictionary. What are the two guide words on the page?

THINK and WRITE

Use what you have learned to complete one of these activities.

1. Pretend your family was in a tornado that wrecked your home. Write a thank you letter to the people who came to help.

2. Imagine that you are a reporter. Write a newspaper story about a tornado. Tell when and where it happened. Explain what it was like and what damage it caused.

3. Look up tornado in the encyclopedia. Find out what you should do in a tornado. Write a list of safety rules.

GETTING READY TO READ

The next story you will read is "Earthquakes." What have you seen, read, and heard about earthquakes? Can you imagine what it would be like to be in an earthquake?

What Do You Think You Will Learn?

Look through "Earthquakes" on pages 26–29. What do you think you will learn when you read this story? Write your ideas below.

_____

_____

_____

_____

_____

_____

EARTHQUAKES

What Are Earthquakes?

In some parts of the world without any warning, the ground may suddenly begin to shake or crack open. The shaking may last for a minute or more and can cause a lot of damage. Buildings may fall and people may be killed. This is an earthquake. It happens when rocks under the land or ocean begin to move.

What Causes Earthquakes?

The Earth seems solid and still, but it is not. Below its surface it is so hot that some rocks melt. The hard crust on the outside of the Earth is the ground we live on. It is cracked in places. The cracks are called faults. Rocks may suddenly slip along a fault and cause an earthquake.

Some faults run across the land. Rocks move sideways along these faults.

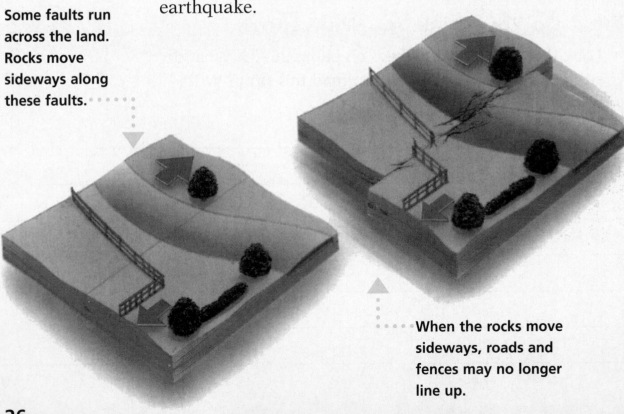

When the rocks move sideways, roads and fences may no longer line up.

How Strong Are Earthquakes?

There are about 500,000 earthquakes every year. Most of them are so small that people do not notice them. Many are under the ocean far from land. About one earthquake in every five is felt by people. A thousand earthquakes cause damage each year. A few very strong ones do a great deal of harm.

In January 1994 an earthquake hit Los Angeles, California. Its strong movements caused buildings like this one a great deal of damage.

Earthquake Zones

The strongest earthquakes are found in earthquake zones. These are the places where huge pieces of the Earth's cracked crust are moving. The pieces of crust are called plates. They fit together like a jigsaw puzzle, but are shifted around by the movements of hot liquid rock inside the Earth.

Hot rock rose from the seafloor and formed a new island called Surtsey.

Earthquakes Under the Ocean

Many mountains rise from the seafloor. They may form long mountain ranges that are hidden beneath the waves. In the middle of the ranges are deep valleys. These are the edges of the Earth's plates. The plates are moving slowly apart. When they move, the seafloor shakes. Hot, runny rock rises from inside the Earth to fill any cracks.

Earthquakes on Land

The edges of most of the moving plates are hidden under the ocean, but some of them are on land. The edge of two plates runs through California. It is a long crack in the ground called the San Andreas Fault. Movements of the plates along this fault cause earthquakes felt in the cities of Los Angeles and San Francisco.

Animals and Earthquakes

In China scientists have noticed that animals often behave strangely before an earthquake. Chickens and horses run around frightened. Pandas moan, and snakes come out of the ground. Perhaps the animals can feel things happening inside the Earth that we cannot feel.

Bridges may collapse in an earthquake.

Earthquake Damage

Earthquakes may shake buildings and bridges until they fall down. People are sometimes buried under the rubble. Another danger is fire because gas pipes may break or stoves may fall over. Fire fighters and other rescue services help people after an earthquake.

From *Earthquakes,* by Keith Lye

AFTER READING

What Did You Learn?

You have read "Earthquakes" for the first time. Now look back at what you wrote on page 25. Did you learn what you thought you would learn? What were you surprised to learn? Write your answers below.

_____

_____

_____

Check Your Understanding

Darken the circle next to the word or words that best complete each sentence.

1. When pieces of the Earth's cracked crust jam together, they cause _____.

    Ⓐ winds   Ⓒ buildings

    Ⓑ rocks   Ⓓ earthquakes

2. The hard crust of the Earth is cracked in places called _____.

    Ⓐ waves   Ⓒ faults

    Ⓑ plates   Ⓓ rocks

3. Pieces of crust called _____ fit together like a puzzle.

    Ⓐ plates   Ⓒ faults

    Ⓑ zones   Ⓓ models

4. The _____ Fault is a long crack in the ground that runs through California.

    Ⓐ Los Angeles   Ⓒ San Francisco

    Ⓑ San Andreas   Ⓓ China

Vocabulary — Context Clues

You can sometimes figure out the meaning of a word by looking at other words around it. You can find the meaning of the word fault by looking at the words and sentences around it.

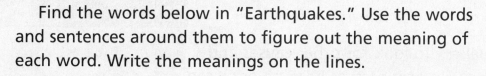

> The hard crust on the outside of the Earth is the ground we live on. It is cracked in places. The cracks are called faults.

From these words and sentences, you can tell that faults are cracks in the Earth's crust.

Find the words below in "Earthquakes." Use the words and sentences around them to figure out the meaning of each word. Write the meanings on the lines.

1. damage (page 26)_____

2. earthquake (page 26) _____

3. rubble (page 29) _____

4. rescue (page 29) _____

Choose one of the words above. Use it in a sentence of your own.

5. _____

_____

Words That Were New to You

Choose words from the story that were new to you. Use a dictionary to check the meanings. Add the words and their meanings to your word list on page 128.

REREADING

Cause and Effect

Sometimes one thing makes another thing happen. What happens is called the effect. What makes it happen is called the cause. Read this sentence from "Earthquakes."

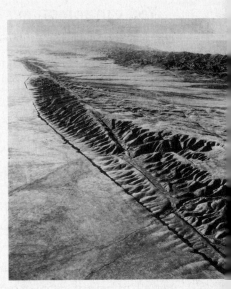

> Rocks may suddenly slip along a fault and cause an earthquake.

In this sentence rocks may suddenly slip along a fault is the cause. An earthquake is the effect.

Reread "Earthquakes" to look for other causes and effects. Looking for clue words such as because or so can help you. As you read, you can ask yourself "What happened?" and "Why did it happen?" What happened is the effect. Why it happened is the cause.

Being able to spot causes and effects will help you be a better reader. You will be able to tell why things happen and predict what will happen next.

After you reread "Earthquakes," complete this cause and effect chart.

Cause (Why did it happen?)	Effect (What happened?)
rocks slip along a fault	earthquake
	danger of fire
movements of plates along the San Andreas fault	
	the seafloor shakes

Compare and Contrast

Use the story and what you know about earthquakes to answer these questions.

1. How are earthquakes on land the same as earthquakes

   under the ocean? _____

   _____

2. How are they different? _____

   _____

STUDY SKILLS

Use an Encyclopedia

You can find more information about earthquakes in an encyclopedia. An encyclopedia has information about people, places, events, and important facts.

Match guide letters with the first letter of your topic. If your topic is earthquakes, choose the volume marked E.

These rules can help you use an encyclopedia.

▶ Use the numbered books, or volumes, to find your topic. Check the guide letters on the volumes.

▶ Match the first letter of your topic with the guide letters. If your topic is earthquakes, choose the encyclopedia book marked E.

▶ Look up people's names under the last name. Choose the M volume to look up Nelson Mandela.

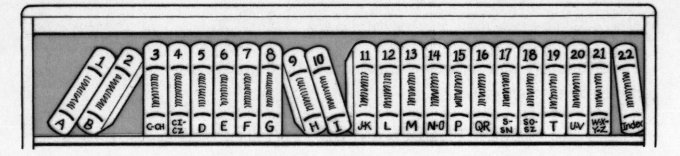

Use what you know about the encyclopedia to answer these questions. Write the number of the correct volume on the line.

_____ **1.** In which volume would you look for facts about China?

_____ **2.** In which volume would you look to find out about the San Francisco earthquake of 1906?

_____ **3.** A machine can measure how strong an earthquake is. This machine was invented by Luigi Palmieri. In which volume would you look to find out about Luigi Palmieri?

Check Yourself

Pick one of your answers. Get that encyclopedia book. Is the topic you thought you would find in that book?

THINK and WRITE

Use what you have learned to complete one of these activities.

1. Suppose you met someone who had never heard of earthquakes. How would you explain earthquakes to that person? Write what you would say.

2. Pretend you are a newspaper reporter. Find out about the San Francisco earthquake of 1906. Write a news story about it.

GETTING READY TO READ

You have read about three kinds of natural disasters. In this story, you will read about a natural disaster that happened a long time ago.

What Do You Think You Will Learn?

Look through "Mt. Vesuvius" on pages 36–38. What kind of natural disaster do you think happened at Mt. Vesuvius? Write your ideas on the lines below.

_____

_____

_____

_____

_____

_____

Mt. Vesuvius

What Is a Volcano?

A volcano is an opening in the earth. Hot, melted rock from inside the earth may escape from this opening. This hot rock is called lava. A volcano might be quiet for hundreds of years. Then, after a long, long time, the volcano blows up again.

What Is Mt. Vesuvius?

Mt. Vesuvius is a mountain with a volcano inside. The mountain is in the south of Italy. Thousands of years ago, people built many towns and farms near it.

The city of Pompeii was built on the foothills near Mt. Vesuvius. This beautiful city looked over the Mediterranean Sea. Pompeii was a busy city. Many people lived in it. Then, on a summer morning almost 2,000 years ago, something terrible happened.

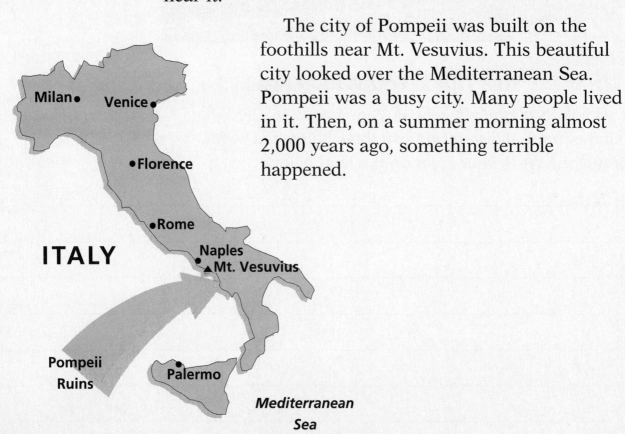

Milan

Venice

Florence

Rome

ITALY

Naples

Mt. Vesuvius

Pompeii Ruins

Palermo

Mediterranean Sea

The Day Pompeii Was Lost

On that summer morning, Mt. Vesuvius began to blow out gases and rock. By early afternoon, the top of the mountain split open. The noise was terrible. A black cloud rose from the volcano. Rock and ash filled the air. For two days ash fell like black snow over everything.

In Pompeii fires broke out. People ran from the city. But 2,000 people stayed behind. They all died. Three days later, the sun came out again. Pompeii was buried under 25 feet of ash, lava, and mud. The nearby towns were also covered.

Later people came back to get their things. They dug through ash and mud. They didn't find much. They finally gave up and moved away. Pompeii was soon forgotten. Hundreds of years passed.

Almost 2,000 years ago, Mt. Vesuvius first blew up. It covered the city of Pompeii in lava and ash.

A City Found Again

More than 1,500 years after Pompeii was buried, a worker began digging a well near Mt. Vesuvius. Instead of finding water, he found the ruins of a town.

People began to dig at the place where Pompeii had been. Over time much of the lost city was dug up. Much of the digging was done by scientists who study old ruins. These scientists are called archaeologists. Archaeologists dug up the marketplace, or forum. They dug up large houses where rich people had lived. They also dug up smaller houses where poor people had lived.

What Can We Learn From Pompeii?

Today people from all over the world visit the ruins at Pompeii. They learn how people lived almost 2,000 years ago.

The things dug up at Pompeii show just how people left them behind. They help visitors to picture everyday life long ago. Visitors can see paintings, furniture, tools, coins, and jewelry from 2,000 years ago. They can walk in and out of houses that are 2,000 years old. In one house, the table is set with silver cups. Maybe guests were coming for supper just before Mt. Vesuvius blew!

Today people can visit the ruins at the city of Pompeii. They can learn how people lived in the past.

AFTER READING

What Did You Learn?

You have read "Mt. Vesuvius" for the first time. Now look back at what you wrote on page 35. What was most interesting about the story? Write two or three ideas below.

_____

_____

_____

Check Your Understanding

Read each sentence. Look at the words in the box. Choose one to complete each sentence. Write the word or words on the correct line.

archaeologists	Mt. Vesuvius
lava ruins	volcano

1. A _____ is an opening in the earth.

2. Hot, melted rock from inside the earth is called

   _____.

3. Pompeii was built near _____.

4. Digging at Pompeii was done by scientists called

   _____.

5. Visitors can see how people lived long ago by visiting

   the _____ at Pompeii.

Vocabulary — Multiple Meanings

Some words have more than one meaning. Fall can mean "a season of the year" or "a drop." Sentence clues can help you understand which meaning is used in a sentence. Read this sentence from the story.

A black cloud rose from the volcano.

The word rose has more than one meaning. It can mean "a flower." It can mean "went up." Look at the word cloud. Clouds belong in the sky. That gives you a clue that rose means "went up."

Read the sentences below. Darken the circle next to the word or words that best tell the meaning of the word in dark print.

1. The **top** of Mt. Vesuvius split open.
   - Ⓐ highest point
   - Ⓒ lid
   - Ⓑ a child's toy
   - Ⓓ best part

2. A cloud can **block** the sun.
   - Ⓐ a child's toy
   - Ⓒ a street
   - Ⓑ hide
   - Ⓓ a piece of wood

3. In 1709 a worker was digging a **well** near Mt. Vesuvius.
   - Ⓐ healthy
   - Ⓒ deep hole for water
   - Ⓑ in a good way
   - Ⓓ clearly

4. In one house, the table is **set** with silver cups.
   - Ⓐ fix clock on time
   - Ⓒ put things in place
   - Ⓑ has TV shows
   - Ⓓ group of things

Words That Were New to You

Choose some words from the story that were new to you. Use a dictionary to check the meanings. Add the words and their meanings to your word list on page 128.

REREADING

Word Referents

Pronouns are words that can replace nouns. They stand for the names of people, places, and things that have already been used. The words in the box are pronouns that can replace nouns.

I	me	you	he
she	it	we	they

Read these sentences from the story.

> But 2,000 people stayed behind. They all died.

The pronoun they stands for the noun people.

Read these sentences. Underline the pronoun. Circle the noun it stands for.

1. A volcano may be quiet for many years, but it can blow up at any time.

2. Mt. Vesuvius has been quiet for a long time. But it might blow up again some day.

3. Scientists like to watch volcanoes blowing up. They like to learn new things about volcanoes.

Reread "Mt. Vesuvius." Watch for pronouns and the nouns they stand for. Then, find a sentence with a pronoun. Find the noun that the pronoun stands for. Write the sentence or sentences on the lines below. Underline the pronoun. Circle the noun.

_____

_____

Cause and Effect

Sometimes one thing makes another thing happen. The effect is what happens. The cause is what makes it happen. Complete the cause and effect chart. You can use the story to help you.

Cause (Why did it happen?)	Effect (What happened?)
The mountain split open. (page 37)	
	Ash fell like black snow over everything. (page 37)
People began to dig where Pompeii had been. (page 38)	

STUDY SKILLS

Diagram

A diagram is a kind of drawing. It shows how something works. Look at this diagram. It shows what happens when a volcano blows up.

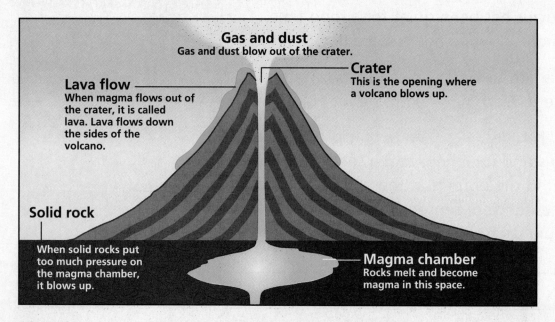

Gas and dust
Gas and dust blow out of the crater.

Crater
This is the opening where a volcano blows up.

Lava flow
When magma flows out of the crater, it is called lava. Lava flows down the sides of the volcano.

Solid rock
When solid rocks put too much pressure on the magma chamber, it blows up.

Magma chamber
Rocks melt and become magma in this space.

Answer each question below. Use the diagram of the volcano to help you.

1. Where is the opening of a volcano?

_____

2. What causes a volcano to blow up?

_____

3. Lava flows out of a volcano. What else blows out?

_____

4. Where does the lava flow?

_____

Check Yourself

Find a diagram in your social studies book. What does it tell about?

THINK and WRITE

Use what you have learned to complete one of these activities.

1. Imagine that you lived in Pompeii 2,000 years ago. Write a story about the day Mt. Vesuvius blew up.

2. You just visited the ruins of Pompeii. Write a letter to your pen pal about your trip.

3. Find out more about Pompeii. You can look up Pompeii in the encyclopedia or find some other books in the library. Write about one of the buildings that was dug up.

2

NEVER GIVE UP!

How can you reach a goal?

Some people make plans and stick to them. They have goals and they work hard to make their dreams come true. They never give up!

Sometimes goals are hard to reach. As you read the stories in this unit, you will learn more about people who have goals that are hard to reach. You will learn how they never give up.

What Do You Already Know?

Think about a person you have read or heard about who would not give up. What were that person's goals? How did the person reach those goals? Write a paragraph that tells how the person stuck to it.

_____

_____

_____

_____

_____

_____

_____

What Do You Want to Find Out?

This unit is about people who never give up. You will read about a man who worked hard to get an education. You will read about a family that worked hard going West. What would you like to learn about these people? On the lines below, write some questions you want answered. You may find the answers to your questions as you read.

_____

_____

_____

_____

_____

_____

GETTING READY TO READ

The first story you are going to read in this unit is "¡Viva México!" What do you know about Mexico? What do you know about its history?

What Do You Think You Will Learn?

Look through "¡Viva México!" Part 1, on pages 47–49. What do you think you will learn when you read this part of the story? How do the pictures help you? Write your ideas below.

_____

_____

_____

_____

_____

_____

¡Viva México!

PART 1

High in the mountains of Mexico was a tiny, adobe house. Its floors were dirt, and it had almost no furniture. It was a poor house in a poor village.

In one of its two rooms, Josefa and Rosa Juárez waited. They knew that soon they would have a new brother or sister.

Then the girls heard a faint wail. The baby! They rushed into Mamá's room. Proudly, she showed them their new brother. How tiny he was.

Mamá and Papá called the baby Benito. They never dreamed that one day all Mexico would know his name.

The Juárez family, like their neighbors, were Zapotec Indians. Few of the Zapotecs spoke Spanish, Mexico's main language. Fewer could read or write. They were so poor that the village had no school.

When Benito was only three, both his parents died. So his grandparents took in the Juárez children. For eight years they raised them. But when Benito was about eleven, his grandparents died. So he went to a nearby village to live with his Uncle Bernardino.

Benito helped his Uncle Bernardino. He watched his uncle's sheep. While Benito made sure the sheep did not wander away, his uncle worked in the cornfield.

Uncle Bernardino knew how to read, and he wanted Benito to learn how, too. So whenever he could, Uncle Bernardino taught Benito.

Soon Benito had learned as much as his uncle could teach him. To learn more, he would have to go to school. But the nearest schools were almost forty miles away in the city of Oaxaca (wuh HAH kuh).

Benito set out for the city without a horse or a burro to ride. He walked across miles of rocky fields and over dusty dirt roads. He grew tired and hungry. But he kept going. At last, he saw the city of Oaxaca.

Benito was amazed. Compared to his tiny village, Oaxaca was huge! Everywhere there were large buildings. The streets were full of people. Benito did not think there were so many people in the whole world. Yet here they were all in one city.

Benito found his way to the house where his sister worked as a cook. Josefa was glad to see Benito. But she could not pay for his schooling. Benito would have to work to pay for school.

Benito went to work for a bookbinder who needed a helper. In return, the bookbinder paid for Benito's schooling. At last Benito could go to a real school!

In Part 2 of "¡Viva México!" you will learn more about the life of Benito Juárez.

AFTER READING

What Did You Learn?

You have read "¡Viva México!" Part 1, for the first time. Now look back at what you wrote on page 46. What was the most interesting thing you learned about Benito Juárez? Write your answer on the lines below.

_____

_____

_____

Check Your Understanding

Darken the circle next to the word or words that best complete each sentence.

1. The new Juárez baby was named _____.

   Ⓐ Benny   Ⓒ Josefa

   Ⓑ Benito   Ⓓ Rosa

2. The Juárez family and most of the people in their village were _____ Indians.

   Ⓐ Spanish   Ⓒ Oaxaca

   Ⓑ French   Ⓓ Zapotec

3. Benito learned how to read from _____.

   Ⓐ Uncle Bernardino   Ⓒ his sister Josefa

   Ⓑ the bookbinder   Ⓓ his grandparents

4. Benito walked across rocky fields to reach _____.

   Ⓐ Zapotec   Ⓒ Oaxaca

   Ⓑ Mexico City   Ⓓ Spain

Vocabulary — Context Clues

When you read stories, you may find new words you don't know. You can use other words or sentences in the story to help you figure out the meanings. Read these sentences from the story.

> Compared to his tiny village, Oaxaca was huge! Everywhere there were large buildings. The streets were full of people. Benito did not think there were so many people in the whole world. Yet here they were all in one city.

The word huge may be new to you. You can figure it out by looking at the sentences around huge. Oaxaca had large buildings. It had many people. These are clues that Oaxaca was big. So huge probably means "big."

Read the sentence. Underline the word or words that tell what the word in dark print means.

1. Benito walked to Oaxaca because he did not have a horse or **burro** to ride.

   a. donkey   **b.** cat   **c.** dog

2. Benito was **amazed** when he saw Oaxaca. He had never seen such large buildings before.

   a. sorry   **b.** surprised   **c.** tired

3. Benito made sure the sheep stayed in the field. He did not want them to **wander.**

   a. stay   **b.** leave   **c.** eat grass

Words That Were New to You

Choose words from the story that were new to you. Use a dictionary to check the meanings. Add the words and their meanings to your word list on page 128.

REREADING

Drawing Conclusions

Writers don't always tell you everything that is happening in a story. Readers often have to use story clues and what they already know to help them. This is called drawing conclusions. Read these story clues about Benito Juárez's first years.

CLUE: When Benito was three, both his parents died.

CLUE: Then he was raised by his grandparents.

CLUE: When he was about eleven, his grandparents died.

The author doesn't tell what Benito's early life was like. You know that his parents died and then his grandparents died, too. You can use these clues to draw a conclusion. His early life must have been hard.

Reread "¡Viva México!" Part 1. Use what you know and clues in the story to help you answer the questions. Circle the best answer. Then, find two story clues that helped you. Write them on the lines.

1. The Juárez family

   a. was very poor.   **c.** lived in a big city.

   b. all went to school.

   CLUE: _____

   CLUE: _____

2. Benito's Uncle Bernardino made a living

   a. as a reading teacher.   **c.** working in Oaxaca.

   b. as a farmer.

   CLUE: _____

   CLUE: _____

Word Referents

Nouns are words that name a person, place, or thing. Pronouns stand for nouns. Read the two sentences below. Then, circle the noun that the pronoun in dark print stands for.

1. Josefa and Rosa rushed into Mamá's room. Proudly, **she** showed them their new brother.

2. Benito was amazed at his first sight of Oaxaca. Compared to his tiny village of 150 people, **it** was huge.

STUDY SKILLS

Table of Contents

A table of contents is found at the beginning of a book. It helps you use the book. A table of contents lists the name of each chapter and the page each chapter starts on. By reading the name of the chapter, you can tell what the chapter is about.

Read this table of contents. Then, use it to answer the questions.

1. What is Chapter 1 about?

    _____

2. Which chapter starts on page 65?

    _____

3. What is Chapter 3 about?

    _____

4. Which chapter starts on page 15?

    _____

Read this table of contents. Then, use it to answer the questions.

5. What chapter starts on page 15?

_____

6. What is Chapter 4 about?

_____

7. What chapter is about tornadoes?

_____

Check Yourself

Find a library book with a table of contents. Find the page number of a chapter you might like to read. Turn to that chapter in the book. Is the chapter about what you thought it would be?

THINK and WRITE

Use what you have learned to complete one of these activities.

1. What would you like to ask Benito Juárez? Write three questions. Then, answer the questions the way you think he would.

2. Imagine you are Benito Juárez, and you like to write about your life in your journal. Tell about the day you left your uncle's home for Oaxaca.

3. Give Benito Juárez an award. Draw a picture of it, and tell why he never gives up.

GETTING READY TO READ

You have read "¡Viva México!" Part 1. What do you like about Benito Juárez? How do you think he sticks to his plans? What do you think he will do next?

What Do You Think You Will Learn?

Look through "¡Viva México!" Part 2, on pages 56–59. Look at the pictures. What else do you think you will learn about Benito Juárez? What else do you think he will do? Write your ideas on the lines below.

_____

_____

_____

_____

_____

_____

_____

¡Viva México!

Benito went to school for many years. He learned reading, writing, history, science, and even law. In 1831, he became a lawyer. He was 25 years old.

As a lawyer, he often took the cases of poor people who could not pay him. They knew they could trust Benito Juárez to do his best.

But Benito Juárez wanted to help even more people. He could not do this just as a lawyer. He decided to work in the government.

Benito Juárez was chosen for many government posts in the state of Oaxaca. Finally, he became the state's governor.

He wanted all children to have a chance to learn to read. So he helped to open more than forty schools in poor villages like his own.

Juárez did many things for the people of Oaxaca. He especially wanted to help Oaxaca's Indians. "I am an Indian and I do not forget my own people," he said.

Benito Juárez was a good governor. The people decided that he would be a good President of Mexico. In 1861, Benito Juárez became President of Mexico.

But Juárez became President during a dangerous time. Far away, in France, the French Emperor decided to try to take over Mexico. He sent soldiers across the sea to fight the Mexican people. The year was 1862.

The French soldiers thought they would have an easy time in Mexico. They were sure that they were stronger than the Mexican soldiers.

The Mexicans got word that the French army was marching through Mexico. High in the hills, the Mexicans waited for the French troops. On the morning of *Cinco de Mayo*—May 5—the Mexicans saw the French soldiers reach the city of Puebla.

They saw thousands of French soldiers on horseback. Thousands more marched on foot. The soldiers' rifles stuck up like a forest of prickly spikes. Horses pulled huge, heavy cannon over the bumpy ground.

The French soldiers looked tired after their long march. The Mexicans began to believe that they had a chance to win.

At about noon the battle began. The French thought the battle would be over quickly. But to their surprise, the Mexicans fought hard and well. After two hours, the armies were still fighting.

By afternoon, the French were running out of bullets and cannon shells. Many soldiers on both sides were dead or wounded. Finally, the French rode away.

The Mexicans had won. *¡Viva México!* Now they knew that they were strong. Now they knew that they had a chance to beat the French.

The French Emperor was angry at the news of the battle of *Cinco de Mayo*. He sent 30,000 more soldiers to Mexico. Soon, they took over Mexico City.

President Juárez had to flee the city. But he waited until the Mexican flag came down from the flagpole. As the flag was lowered, a band played the Mexican national anthem.

President Juárez took the flag in his hands and kissed it. *"¡Viva México!"* he cried. Then he rode away into the hills.

For five years, the French ruled Mexico. But Benito Juárez and the other Mexican leaders kept fighting. They never gave up.

At last, in 1867, they won. The French left. Mexico was free again. From that time on, no other country has ever ruled Mexico.

President Juárez rode back into Mexico City. He raised the Mexican flag. *"¡Viva México!"* he cried.

"¡Viva México! ¡Viva Juárez!" the people shouted.

From *¡Viva México!* by Argentina Palacios

AFTER READING

What Did You Learn?

You have read "¡Viva México!" Part 2, for the first time. Now look back at what you wrote on page 55. What did you learn that you thought you would learn? What did you learn that was new? Write your answers on the lines below.

_____

_____

_____

Check Your Understanding

Darken the circle next to the word or words that best complete each sentence.

1. Benito studied in Oaxaca to become a _____.

    Ⓐ farmer   Ⓒ teacher

    Ⓑ scientist   Ⓓ lawyer

2. In time, Benito became the state governor of _____.

    Ⓐ his village   Ⓒ France

    Ⓑ Oaxaca   Ⓓ Spain

3. On Cinco de Mayo, French and Mexican soldiers fought at _____.

    Ⓐ Oaxaca   Ⓒ Paris

    Ⓑ Puebla   Ⓓ Mexico City

4. In 1867, after _____ years of French rule, Mexico was free!

    Ⓐ five   Ⓒ fifty

    Ⓑ ten   Ⓓ one hundred

Vocabulary — Synonyms and Antonyms

Synonyms are words that mean almost the same thing. Read this sentence. The words in dark print are synonyms.

French troops were fighting Mexican soldiers.

Antonyms are words that have opposite meanings. Read this sentence. The words in dark print are antonyms.

The French defeat was a great win for Mexico.

Look at the words in dark print in these sentences. If the words are synonyms, write an S on the line. If they are antonyms, write an A.

_____ 1. At noon the **battle** started. By evening, the **fight** was over.

_____ 2. The Mexicans thought they were **weak** and the French were **strong.**

_____ 3. The French emperor was **angry.** He was so **mad** that he sent 30,000 more soldiers to Mexico.

_____ 4. The French soldiers were **tired.** But the Mexicans were **rested** and ready.

_____ 5. The people **shouted,** "¡Viva Juárez!" when they saw the President. They **yelled** for a long time.

_____ 6. The Mexicans finally **won.** The French had **lost.**

Words That Were New to You

Choose words from the story that were new to you. Use a dictionary to check the meanings. Add the words and their meanings to your word list on page 128.

REREADING

Sequence

Many stories are told in the order that things take place. The things that happen in the story are called events. Keeping track of events can help you remember the story. Use words like first, then, next, and last or finally. Look at this chart. It shows what Benito did in Oaxaca.

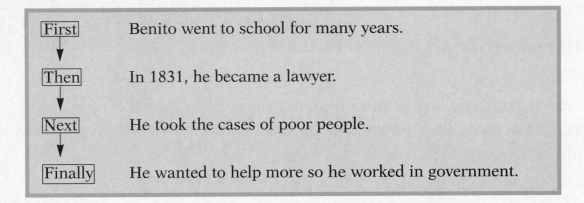

First — Benito went to school for many years.

Then — In 1831, he became a lawyer.

Next — He took the cases of poor people.

Finally — He wanted to help more so he worked in government.

Read "¡Viva México!" Part 2, again. As you go along, finish the chart below. It shows what happened after Juárez was president.

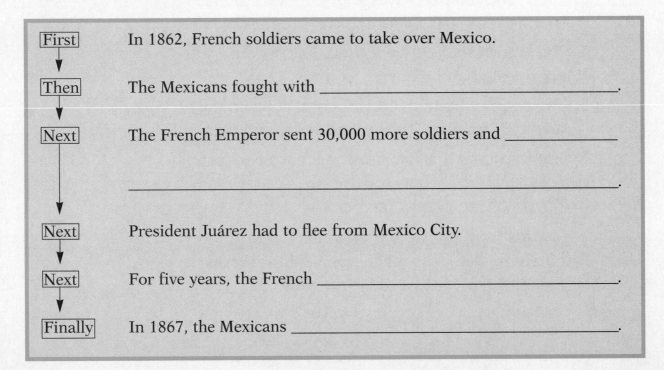

First — In 1862, French soldiers came to take over Mexico.

Then — The Mexicans fought with _____.

Next — The French Emperor sent 30,000 more soldiers and _____

_____.

Next — President Juárez had to flee from Mexico City.

Next — For five years, the French _____.

Finally — In 1867, the Mexicans _____.

Drawing Conclusions

Readers often have to use story clues and what they already know to figure out what is happening in a story. This is called drawing conclusions.

Finish this sentence about Benito Juárez. Circle the best answer. Write two story clues that helped you.

Benito Juárez

    a. was a lazy man.

    b. was a great Mexican hero.

    c. was a great fighter.

CLUE: _____

CLUE: _____

STUDY SKILLS

Time Line

You have read about events in Benito Juárez's life. One way to keep track of events in the order they happen is on a time line. Here's how to make one.

  ▶ Start with the first event. Use dates if you can.

  ▶ Mark the events on the time line so they show the right space of time between them.

  ▶ End with the last event.

Early Life of Benito Juárez

| He was born in a village. | His parents died. | He went to his uncle's village. | He moved to Oaxaca. |

The time line below has dates on it. The numbers on the time line go with the questions. Go back to the story to help you complete the time line.

Later Life of Benito Juárez

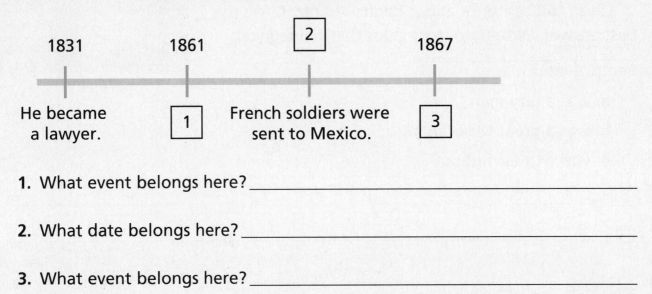

1831   1861   2   1867

He became a lawyer.   1   French soldiers were sent to Mexico.   3

1. What event belongs here? _____

2. What date belongs here? _____

3. What event belongs here? _____

Check Yourself

Make a time line of your life. How many events will you put on the time line?

THINK and WRITE

Use what you have learned to complete one of these activities.

1. Pretend you are a soldier in Benito Juárez's army. Write about Cinco de Mayo.

2. What do you think Benito Juárez would say to his army before a fight? Write his speech.

3. Write a travel booklet about a place in Mexico. Use the encyclopedia to help.

GETTING READY TO READ

The next story is called "Going West." In it you will read about a pioneer family. They leave their home to make a new one on the prairie. How would you feel about leaving your home and your friends behind?

What Do You Think You Will Learn?

Look through "Going West," Part 1, on pages 66–69. What do you think you will learn in the story? Write your ideas below.

_____

_____

_____

_____

_____

_____

_____

Going West Part 1

One day in early spring we packed everything we had into our wagon, tied our milk cow Sadie on behind, and set out to find a new home.

Going West.

There were five of us: Papa and Mama; me, Hannah; my little brother Jake; and Rebecca, a fat baby with yellow curls.

Mama cried. She was leaving her three sisters and all our furniture and the piano she loved to play. But Papa said we were going to a place where anything you planted would grow and a farm could stretch out as far as the eye could see.

We left behind the town we knew, the woods, the hills. We rode, bouncing and swaying in the creaking wagon, day after day.

At night Mama cooked over a campfire and we slept close together on the wagon floor, with stars winking through the opening in our canvas roof.

Here is what was in our wagon: blankets and pillows and quilts, Mama's favorite rocking chair, trunks full of clothes, barrels full of food, a cookstove, a box of tin dishes, all of Mama's cooking pots, all of Papa's tools, a Bible, a rifle, and a spinning wheel.

There was barely room for us.

Sometimes it rained. Our wagon got stuck in the mud and we all had to get out and push. Once it rained so hard that the wagon leaked. That night we slept in wet clothes in wet beds, without any supper. Rebecca cried, and Jake said he wanted to go home. Mama didn't say anything, but I think she felt the same.

We were all tired of the rocking wagon and the dust and the same sights day after day. Jake fell out and hurt his arm. Rebecca caught a cold. At night she coughed and coughed. Mama looked worried, but still we rode on.

Going West.

We came to a river, all muddy and wide.

"How will we get across?" I asked Papa.

"The horses will take us," he said.

First the water came up to the horses' knees. And then their chests.

Suddenly Papa shouted, "Hold on tight!"

The horses were swimming. Water was pouring into the wagon. Mama held me tight, until at last I felt the horses' feet touch bottom again.

We had crossed the river.

On the other side of the river the land was flat, with no trees. There was not a bush and not a stone; nothing but green, waving grass and blue sky and a constant, whispering wind. It seemed a lonely, empty place.

But Papa said, "This is the land we've been looking for."

As the sun was setting, we came upon a place where wildflowers bloomed in mounds of pink and lavender and blue, like soft pillows.

"Look," said Mama, smiling.

And Papa said, "Here is where we will build our house."

The next day we began. Papa took the horses and rode away. When he came back, he brought logs from the creek. For many days he worked. Slowly, with Mama helping, he built walls, a roof, a door.

Finally he took Mama's rocking chair and set it next to our new fireplace. It was only one room, with dirt for a floor, but at last we slept in a house again.

Mama planted a garden. Jake carried water from the creek to do the washing. I minded the baby and swept the dirt floor and helped Mama hang checked curtains on the window.

"There," she said. "We are ready for visitors."

But no visitors came. We were alone on the vast prairie.

Papa rode away again, many miles to town. For three long days we watched and waited. And then Papa came back. He brought flour and bacon and six sheep that he traded for one of the horses and a surprise: real white sugar.

Mama baked a cake and it reminded me of home.

In Part 2 of "Going West," you will learn more about Hannah and her family.

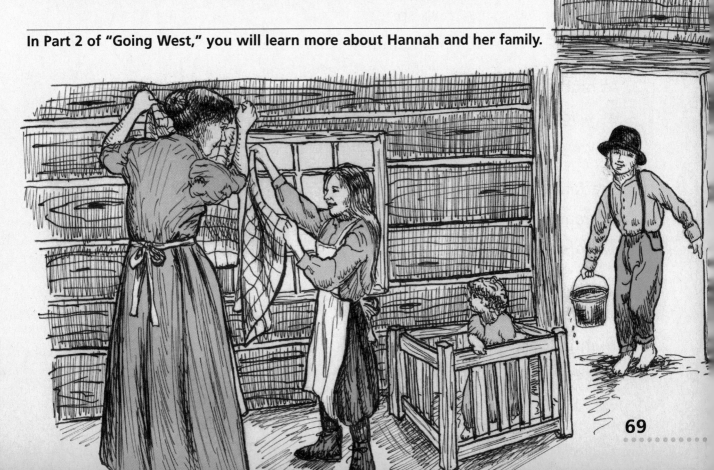

AFTER READING

What Did You Learn?

You have read "Going West," Part 1, for the first time. Look back at what you wrote on page 65. Did you learn what you thought you would learn? What did you learn that surprised you? Write your answers below.

_____

_____

_____

Check Your Understanding

Darken the circle next to the word or words that best complete each sentence.

1. The family packed everything in their wagon and left in early _____.

   Ⓐ winter   Ⓒ spring

   Ⓑ fall   Ⓓ summer

2. At night the family slept together on the _____.

   Ⓐ wagon floor   Ⓒ ground outdoors

   Ⓑ wagon roof   Ⓓ straw mattresses

3. The family crossed the river by _____.

   Ⓐ boat   Ⓒ wagon

   Ⓑ horseback   Ⓓ swimming

4. There were many different _____ where the family built their house.

   Ⓐ mountains   Ⓒ neighbors

   Ⓑ trees   Ⓓ wildflowers

Vocabulary — Contractions

Sometimes two words are put together to make a shorter word. The shorter word is called a contraction. Look at these words.

have not	haven't

Haven't is a contraction for have not. The contraction has an apostrophe in it. The apostrophe looks like this '. It stands for the o in not. Read this sentence from the story.

Mama didn't say anything, but I think she felt the same.

The contraction didn't stands for did not. The apostrophe stands for the letter o in not.

Read these sentences. Circle each contraction. Then write the two words that make up the contraction.

1. The family hadn't slept well on their long trip.

   _____   _____

2. They don't know how long it will take to build their house.

   _____   _____

3. It isn't easy to make a long trip in a wagon.

   _____   _____

Words That Were New to You

Choose words from the story that were new to you. Use a dictionary to check the meanings. Add the words and their meanings to your word list on page 128.

REREADING

Dialogue

The words that characters say to each other in a story are called dialogue. The words have these special marks around them " ". These marks are called quotation marks. Read this sentence from the story.

> **Suddenly Papa shouted, "Hold on tight!"**

In this sentence, "Hold on tight!" is the dialogue. You can tell because the words are in quotation marks. They are the words that Papa says.

Reread "Going West," Part 1. Find the clues that tell when someone is speaking.

After you reread "Going West," Part 1, read the sentences below. Circle the words that are dialogue. Then, on the line write the name of the person who is talking.

1. "This is the land we've been looking for," Papa said.

   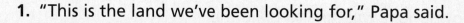

2. "Look," said Mama, smiling.

   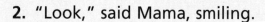

3. And Papa said, "Here is where we will build our house."

   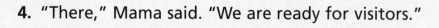

4. "There," Mama said. "We are ready for visitors."

Sequence

The order of the things that happen in a story is called
sequence. Read each sentence. Then, tell what happened
next. Use the story to help you.

1. The pioneer family came to a muddy river.

   Next:_____

2. Papa came back with logs from the creek.

   Next:_____

STUDY SKILLS

Dictionary — Pronunciation Key

When you read a new word in the dictionary, you can
find a pronunciation key right after the word. This can
help you learn how to say a word.

Look at this part of a dictionary page and
pronunciation key.

sleep (slēp) v. rest one's body and mind.

sleigh (slā) n. carriage on runners for
travel on snow or ice.

slide (slīd) v. move smoothly, like a sled.

Pronunciation Key	
a	hat
ā	tape
e	let
ē	be
i	bit
ī	mice

Look at the word sleep. The letters slēp are in
parentheses. Parentheses look like this ( ). The letters tell
you how to say sleep. Look at the pronunciation key. It
shows you that an e with a line over the top has the long
e sound you hear in be.

Use what you know to finish each sentence. Use the pronunciation key to find the answer. Circle the answer.

1. The ee in sleep sounds like the

   e in be   e in let

2. The i in spike sounds like the

   i in bit   i in mice

3. The a in camp sounds like the

   a in hat   a in tape

4. The i in rifle sounds like the

   i in bit   i in mice

Pronunciation Key	
a	hat
ā	tape
e	let
ē	be
i	bit
ī	mice

Check Yourself

Look up a new word in the dictionary. Check how to say it. Say the word to a friend.

THINK and WRITE

Use what you have learned to complete one of these activities.

1. Imagine that you were with the pioneer family in "Going West." Write in your journal about one day of your trip.

2. You have just settled down after a wagon trip to the prairie. Write a postcard to a friend back home. Draw a picture on the front of the postcard.

3. Make a list of what you would take on a wagon trip out West. Pack lightly, but list what you would need.

4. Look at a map of your country. Pick a place you would like to visit. Write a story about a trip there with your family.

GETTING READY TO READ

The next story you are going to read is "Going West," Part 2. Think about what you read in Part 1 of this story. How would you feel if your family were going West? What would you do in a new land?

What Do You Think You Will Learn?

Look through "Going West," Part 2, on pages 76–80. What do you think happens to the pioneer family in their new home? Will they learn to like it? Write your ideas below.

_____

_____

_____

_____

_____

_____

_____

Going West Part 2

Summer came. A hot wind blew. Papa went out hunting for rabbits, and Jake and I picked blackberries next to the creek.

Mama lay down in the grass with the sheep.

"Oh my," she sighed when we found her. "This is a lonesome land."

Day after day the sun beat down, baking our little house, shriveling up the plants in the garden. It was so hot that nothing moved, not even the wind.

"If only we had a tree for shade," said Mama.

One afternoon when Jake and I were at the creek, dark clouds suddenly covered the sun. Thunder rumbled and lightning flashed. We ran for home. But before we got there, hail came tumbling out of the sky, big and round and hard as marbles.

"Quick!" I shouted. "The buckets!" We put them over our heads and kept running.

Mama was waiting at the door. "Thank goodness you're safe," she said.

When the storm was over, Mama's garden was squashed flat. "The land is good," she said. "But the weather is hard."

"Never mind," said Papa. "In the spring we will plant again."

Mama was frying donuts and Jake and I were doing our lessons on the dirt floor, when visitors finally came: Indians! Jake hid under the bed. I crept behind the rocking chair, my knees trembling with fright. They looked so fierce.

But Mama smiled. She gave one of the Indians a donut. The Indian smiled. Mama kept on making donuts and the Indians kept on eating donuts until Papa came home. And then the Indians went away.

The wind turned cold. Mama stored up potatoes and berries and nuts for the long winter to come. Papa went hunting for deer. He came back with Mr. Swenson. Mr. Swenson stayed for supper and afterward he played his flute while Mama sang, sitting around the fire. And suddenly the prairie wasn't empty anymore.

We had a neighbor.

"Do they have Christmas out here?" Jake asked. And I wondered too.

But Mama said, "Of course."

So we hung our stockings by the chimney. Rebecca got a cup and Jake a whistle and I found Nelly, a rag doll with yellow braids. Later we had wild turkey for dinner and Mama opened the jam she had been saving all year.

And everything was just like Christmas.

Now the icy wind seeped through cracks in our log walls. We put on all the clothes we had and huddled next to the fire. One morning it was so cold that Mama's fresh-baked bread was frozen solid. And then it began to snow.

It snowed for three days and three nights. Papa tied a rope from the house to the stable so he could feed the animals.

Jake and I did our lessons and Mama helped me sew on my quilt and we all listened to the wind howling outside.

At last everything grew still. Looking out, we saw no woodpile, no stable, no sky, nothing but snow drifting up to the roof of our little house.

It was a long, cold winter. We had nothing to eat but potatoes and hard biscuits and nuts. Rebecca cried because she was hungry. And one day Mama counted the potatoes and said, "There are only six left."

But then slowly the snow began to melt. Each day the drifts under our window grew smaller. Papa took down his rifle and went hunting again. And that night the smell of rabbit stew made our house warm once more.

One morning when the grass was turning new green, Papa said, "It's planting time."

He hitched our horse to the plow and broke through the tough prairie grass to the dark, rich soil beneath. For days he worked, plowing long, straight rows. Then Mama dropped in seeds and Jake and I covered them up. The warm sun shone. The seeds sprouted. And all around us, as far as my eyes could see, was our farm.

It was Mama's birthday. Jake and I picked flowers for the table. Papa brought home a surprise: a little tree from the creek to plant by the front door.

"Next year if the corn does well," he said, "we will buy a piano."

And Mr. Swenson came for dinner with another surprise: his new wife.

"Welcome to our house," said Mama.

We ate Mama's food and listened to Mrs. Swenson tell about back East and sang, sitting around the fire. Outside, a soft wind was blowing in the new corn.

I looked around at Mama in her rocking chair and Rebecca sleeping and Jake leaning on Papa's knee.

And our house felt like home.

From *Going West,* by Jean Van Leeuwen

AFTER READING

What Did You Learn?

You have read the second part of "Going West." Now look back at what you wrote on page 75. Were you surprised by the ending? Why or why not?

_____

_____

_____

Check Your Understanding

Darken the circle next to the word that best completes each sentence.

1. A bad storm ruined Mama's _____.

   Ⓐ garden   Ⓒ sheep

   Ⓑ cabins   Ⓓ clothes

2. When Mr. Swenson arrived, the family was glad to have a _____ nearby.

   Ⓐ store   Ⓒ doctor

   Ⓑ neighbor   Ⓓ singer

3. During the long winter, the family only had _____, hard biscuits, and nuts to eat.

   Ⓐ pies   Ⓒ apples

   Ⓑ corn   Ⓓ potatoes

4. When spring arrived, Papa planted a _____ near the front door.

   Ⓐ chimney   Ⓒ tree

   Ⓑ sunflower   Ⓓ seed

Vocabulary — Prefixes

A prefix is a word part that is added to the beginning of a word. A prefix changes the meaning of a word. Look at these prefixes and their meanings.

un-	means	"not" or "the opposite of"
re-	means	"to do again"

Look at the sentences below.

1. We unpacked the wagon.

2. They will replant the garden next spring.

In sentence 1, unpacked means "the opposite of packed." In sentence 2, replant means "to plant again."

Read each sentence. Draw a circle around each word with a prefix. Then, write the meaning of the word on the line.

1. Papa retied the rope several times.

   _____

2. Mama was unhappy that there weren't more trees.

   _____

3. Mama recounted the potatoes.

   _____

4. Papa was unsure when the snow would stop.

   _____

Words That Were New to You

Choose words from the story that were new to you. Use a dictionary to check the meanings. Add the words and their meanings to your word list on page 128.

82

REREADING

Main Idea and Details

A **main idea** is the most important idea in a paragraph. It tells what the paragraph is about. **Details** tell more about the main idea. Read this paragraph from the story.

> It was Mama's birthday. Jake and I picked flowers for the table. Papa brought home a surprise: a little tree from the creek to plant by the front door.

The first sentence tells the main idea. It was Mama's birthday. The other sentences tell details. They tell the special things the family did for Mama's birthday.

Reread the second part of "Going West." Look for a sentence that tells what each paragraph is about. Sometimes it will be the first sentence. Sometimes it will be in another part of the paragraph.

After you reread the story, write two details that tell more about each main idea below.

1. Main Idea: One afternoon when Jake and I were at the creek, dark clouds suddenly covered the sun. (page 76)

   DETAIL: _____

   DETAIL: _____

2. Main Idea: Now the icy wind seeped through cracks in our log walls. (page 78)

   DETAIL: _____

   DETAIL: _____

Dialogue

Dialogue is what people say to each other in a story.
Use the story to answer the questions below.

1. What is one sentence that Papa says on page 77?

   _____

2. What is one sentence that Mama says on page 80?

   _____

STUDY SKILLS

Library — Fiction and Nonfiction

There are two kinds of books you can find in the library. They are fiction and nonfiction. Knowing the difference will help you find books.

Fiction books are made-up stories. "Going West" is a fiction story. Nonfiction books tell facts about real things, such as floods and volcanoes.

Here are some ideas about the kinds of fiction and nonfiction books you might find in the library.

Fiction	Nonfiction
▶ a made-up story about a super hero *The King-Size Kid*	▶ a true story about a country's hero *¡Viva México!*
▶ a make-believe story about space travel *Adventures on Mars*	▶ a true story about space travel *To the Moon and Back*
▶ a made-up book about silly foods *Big Blue Burgers*	▶ a cookbook about foods the pioneers ate *Pioneer Cooking*

Look at the titles of each book below. Read what the book is about. If the book is fiction, write F on the line. If it is nonfiction, write N.

_____ **1.** *It's Our World, Too.* Stories about real kids doing something to help their world.

_____ **2.** *A Visit to Another Planet.* The make-believe adventures of kids who visit Mars.

_____ **3.** *Those Who Went West.* The story of real people who traveled west in covered wagons.

Check Yourself

Go to the library. Find one fiction book and one nonfiction book about pioneers. Write the titles of the books and tell whether they are fiction or nonfiction.

THINK  and WRITE

Use what you have learned to complete one of these activities.

1. You write for a newspaper. You are going to interview a pioneer woman. List questions to ask her. Write what you think her answers would be.

2. Imagine that you live on the prairie in pioneer days. You're putting away a treasure box for the future. What would you put in the box? Tell why.

3. Find out about the Conestoga wagons that pioneers drove west. Use an encyclopedia or other books to help you. Write a report on your findings.

IT'S YOUR WORLD

How can you keep it clean?

Your living space in the world is called your environment. Air, water, soil, and living things are part of your environment. You need them to live. Sometimes people do things to harm, or pollute, the environment. Cars give off gas that pollutes the air. So do factories. And farmers may use harmful sprays on their crops. As you read, you will learn what you can do to help keep your world clean.

What Do You Already Know?

Did you ever see someone leave trash on the ground? Did you ever think the air smelled really bad? Write a paragraph about a time you saw how people can pollute the environment. Tell what you saw.

_____

_____

_____

_____

_____

_____

_____

What Do You Want to Find Out?

You will find out about ways people harm the air, soil, and water. You will also learn how people can clean up the environment. On the lines below, write some questions you want answered. As you read, you may find the answers to some of these questions.

_____

_____

_____

_____

_____

_____

_____

GETTING READY TO READ

The first story you will read is "Pollution." What do you already know about how people pollute the air, water, and land? Did you ever think about how you could help?

What Do You Think You Will Learn?

Look through "Pollution," Part 1, on pages 89–92. What do you think you will learn when you read this story? Write your ideas below.

_____

_____

_____

_____

_____

_____

POLLUTION

PART 1

All living things need the sun. They need the light and heat from the sun. When the sun warms the soil, plants can grow in it. Animals need these plants for food. And people need plants in many ways. Nothing can live or grow without the sun.

Plants and animals that live in the sea also need the heat of the sun. The warm sea heats the air that is over it. Then the warm air brings water to the land as rain. The rain helps plants grow. But plants also need good soil and clean air to grow.

Every day people hurt the soil. Every day people put poisons into the air. And every day people pour wastes into the water. We call this pollution. We must stop polluting our environment.

All living things need a clean environment. Without sunlight and heat, good soil and plants, or clean air and water, this mountain goat could not live.

All living things depend on one another. They are like links in a chain. If one link is killed, the others may die also.

In the Arctic, tiny plants and animals called plankton live near the top of the water. Fish eat the plankton. Seabirds come to eat the fish. But if pollution kills the fish, the birds won't have food.

The seabirds nest on the land. They leave droppings on the rocks. Then mosses grow on the droppings and plants grow on the dead moss. Next insects feed on the plants. And then small animals feed on the insects. If the seabirds die, other animals and plants also die.

Sometimes farmers cut down trees and bushes. They do this to make room for their crops. When they do this, they destroy the homes of all the animals that depend on the trees and bushes. Wild plants and animals die.

When water gets polluted, many fish die.

90

People cut down trees and pull up plants so grass can grow. When all the trees and plants are gone, there are no big roots to hold down the soil. So the rain washes the best soil away. Without good soil, nothing much can grow.

All over the world more and more people are being born. Farmers must find ways to grow food for all the people. Farmers can find ways to bring water to new land. They can add fertilizers to make plants grow better. They can spray their crops to kill pests.

But using sprays can cause pollution problems. Some sprays that farmers use to kill pests can harm useful animals. Small birds eat pests that have been sprayed. The chemicals from the sprays stay inside the bodies of the birds. The chemicals cause the eggs that the birds lay to have thin shells. These thin shells can easily break.

When farmers use sprays to kill pests, they can cause harm to other animals.

Smoke from buildings is a big pollution problem in some cities.

Air pollution is also a big problem. We often breathe dirty air. Some of the dirt comes from factories and houses that burn gas, coal, and oil. These fuels make smoke that pollutes the air.

Cars pollute the air. The smoke from their engines can form smog. Smog is a mixture of smoke and fog. Smog can hurt people's eyes and lungs. Today all cars must have special pollution tools on them to block the smoke. But car pollution is still a problem because so many cars are on the road.

Polluted air can even poison the rain. Gases in the air make acid in the rainwater. This acid can spoil stone and other building materials.

Polluted air can even spoil farm crops. It can kill trees. If there is a lot of pollution in the air, less light and heat from the sun reaches the earth.

When you read Part 2 of this story, you will find out what people can do to stop pollution.

AFTER READING

What Did You Learn?

You have read "Pollution," Part 1, for the first time. Now look back at what you wrote on page 88. Did you learn anything about pollution that surprised you? Write two or three new things you learned below.

_____

_____

_____

Check Your Understanding

Darken the circle next to the word or words that best complete each sentence.

1. Living things need _____.

   Ⓐ the sun   Ⓒ the mosses

   Ⓑ fertilizers   Ⓓ the roots

2. Smog is caused by a mixture of smoke and _____.

   Ⓐ rain   Ⓒ fog

   Ⓑ air   Ⓓ soil

3. Some pollution comes from factories and houses that burn _____, coal, and oil.

   Ⓐ acid   Ⓒ smoke

   Ⓑ sprays   Ⓓ gas

4. Pollution in the air can stop the _____ from the sun from reaching the earth.

   Ⓐ air and water   Ⓒ poisons and gas

   Ⓑ smoke and fog   Ⓓ light and heat

Vocabulary — Possessives

When you add an apostrophe -s like this 's to a noun, the 's shows ownership. Read this sentence.

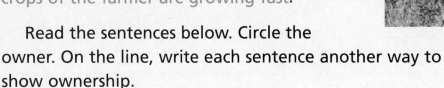

The farmer's crops are growing fast.

You can tell from the 's at the end of farmer that the farmer owns the crops. Another way to write this sentence is The crops of the farmer are growing fast.

Read the sentences below. Circle the owner. On the line, write each sentence another way to show ownership.

1. Smog can hurt people's eyes.

_____

2. The seabird's nest is on land.

_____

3. The animal's home is in the grass.

_____

4. The car's smoke mixes with fog.

_____

5. We need the sun's light and heat.

_____

Words That Were New to You

Choose words from the story that were new to you. Use a dictionary to check the meanings. Add the words and their meanings to your word list on page 128.

REREADING

Fact and Opinion

Writers tell different kinds of ideas in a story. Facts are ideas that are true. A writer can prove they are true. Opinions tell how a writer feels or thinks about something. Read these sentences.

1. Scientists know living things need sun. (fact)

2. Sunny days are the best days. (opinion)

The first sentence is a fact because scientists have proved living things need sun. The second sentence is an opinion. Some people like sunny days and some do not.

Sometimes writers tell when they give an opinion. They use words such as I think, I believe, we should, or in my opinion. Look for these words when you read. They help you tell opinions from facts.

Read each sentence. On the line before the sentence, write F if it is a fact. Write O if it is an opinion.

_____ **1.** I believe seabirds are beautiful birds.

_____ **2.** We should have a law against harmful crop sprays.

_____ **3.** Smog can hurt people's lungs.

_____ **4.** I think air pollution is the biggest problem we have.

_____ **5.** Today all cars must have pollution tools on them to block smoke.

_____ **6.** All living things depend on one another.

Reread Part 1 of "Pollution." Look for clues that tell you the writer is giving an opinion in the story. Then, write two facts you find in the story.

7. _____

8. _____

Main Idea and Details

A main idea tells what a paragraph is all about. Details tell more about the main idea. Write a detail that tells about each main idea below. Use the story to help you.

1. Main Idea: All living things need the sun. (page 89)

   DETAIL: _____

2. Main Idea: The seabirds nest on the land. (page 90)

   DETAIL: _____

3. Main Idea: Cars pollute the air. (page 92)

   DETAIL: _____

STUDY SKILLS

Outline and Take Notes

When you read, you can take notes to help you understand and remember ideas. One way to take notes is to make an outline. An outline shows important ideas and details.

Look at part of an outline below.

1. Many animals live near fields and forests.

   a. Trees and bushes give animals shelter.

   b. Insects eat the leaves, flowers, and seeds.

   c. Birds and animals eat the insects.

The first line of this outline tells an important idea about where animals live. The sentences below give details about the idea. They tell three reasons why animals live near fields and forests.

Complete the outline below. You can look back at the story if you need to. Write on the lines.

1. All living things need sun. (page 89)

   a. The sun warms the soil.

   b. Plants grow in the soil.

   c. _____

2. Air pollution is a big problem. (page 92)

   a. People breathe dirty air.

   b. Some of the dirt comes from factories.

   c. _____

Check Yourself

Make an outline that shows the kinds of pollution where you live. What important ideas did you show?

THINK and WRITE

Use what you have learned to complete one of these activities.

1. Write a story for a class newspaper about the environment. Put your story together with your classmates' stories. Call your class newspaper "Save the Earth!"

2. Make a poster about pollution. Then, think of a title for it and write the title on the poster.

3. Draw a chain showing how living things depend on each other. Use plankton, fish, seabirds, mosses, plants, and insects as links in your chain. Tell how each link helps the other links.

GETTING READY TO READ

You have read the first part of "Pollution." You've learned some ways that people pollute the environment. What are some ways they can help keep it clean? Is there anything you can do about this problem?

What Do You Think You Will Learn?

Look through "Pollution," Part 2, on pages 99–103. What do you think you will find out about pollution in this part? Write your ideas below.

_____

_____

_____

_____

_____

_____

POLLUTION
PART 2

Cars pollute the air in big cities. So people living there must find other ways to move about. Many big cities have subways. Subway trains can carry many people at a time under the streets. Buses can also carry many people. One bus can carry as many people as fifty cars can.

Some places don't let people bring their cars to the center of town. Drivers must leave their cars at the edge of town in a parking lot. Then buses bring them from the parking lot to the center of town.

In large cities, many people drive cars to work, which pollutes the air.

Noise is also a kind of pollution. Very loud noise can make people sick. Noise can hurt people's ears and spoil their hearing.

Many towns bury their garbage in large pits like this one.

Things that people throw away are either junk or garbage. Junk and garbage can cause pollution. Some junk and garbage will rot, but some will not.

Food will rot if it is thrown away. Things made of metal and paper will also rot after a long time. But plastic and rubber will never rot. They give off a poisonous gas when they are burned. A big problem is finding a way to get rid of plastic and rubber junk.

Junk and garbage can be used to fill a pit. They are packed together and then covered with soil. But there are not enough pits for all the things people throw away.

People are now finding ways of using old metals, glass, cloth, and paper again. Using things again is called recycling.

People send wastewater, or sewage, from their homes to rivers and lakes nearby. The water is too dirty to go right to a river. So it is changed at a sewage plant.

At the plant, the sewage goes through screens. The screens catch solid things. The rest of the sewage then flows into big tanks. The dirt drops to the bottom of the tanks. And the sun and air help kill the germs in the water at the top of the tank.

When sewage is dumped without going to a sewage plant, rivers can become polluted. · · · ·

Many towns use water from a river. Wastewater that is cleaned in a sewage plant is dumped into the river. If wastewater is not cleaned, the river can become polluted with poisons and germs.

People are trying to save the environment. They have set aside some lands where only plants and animals can live. No one is allowed to bother the animals. No one is allowed to hurt the plants. Here, living things enjoy their natural home.

Plants and animals live in balance. This means they help each other. This picture shows how water plants and animals live together in balance. Each living thing gets all it needs from the environment.

The plants put oxygen into the water. The animals must take in this oxygen to live. When they do this, they breathe out carbon dioxide gas. Plants then use this carbon dioxide to make food. This is how animals help plants.

An aquarium shows how plants and animals live together in balance.

You can help your environment. You can start a compost heap for your garden. A compost heap is a pile of food scraps, leaves, and anything else that will rot. You can also put weeds and grass clippings on the heap. Then put water on the heap to help it rot. After a few weeks, spread the compost around your garden.

You can help the environment by feeding birds. You can put food on a bird table in cold weather. Birds have trouble finding food in winter.

You can help the environment by recycling your clothes, games, and other things. When you outgrow your clothes, don't throw them away. Give them to someone who can reuse them. Do the same with games that you have outgrown and don't play with anymore.

Helping the environment is really helping yourself, your friends, your family, and the world!

A compost heap can use up food scraps and recycle garbage. Compost can also help a garden grow.

From *Pollution*, by Herta S. Breiter

AFTER READING

What Did You Learn?

You have read "Pollution," Part 2, for the first time. Now look back at what you wrote on page 98. Did you learn what you thought you would learn? What did you learn that was new to you? Write your answers on the lines below.

_____

_____

_____

Check Your Understanding

Darken the circle next to the word or words that best complete each sentence.

1. Very loud noise can _____.

   Ⓐ sound good   Ⓒ make things rot

   Ⓑ make people sick   Ⓓ give off poisonous gas

2. People are finding ways to recycle metals and glass so they can _____.

   Ⓐ be burned   Ⓒ be used again

   Ⓑ rot   Ⓓ be thrown away

3. A pile of food scraps and leaves to use in a garden is a _____ heap.

   Ⓐ compost   Ⓒ garbage

   Ⓑ balance   Ⓓ pit

4. When living things help each other, they live in _____.

   Ⓐ balance   Ⓒ greenhouse

   Ⓑ cold weather   Ⓓ water

Vocabulary — Multiple Meanings

Many words have more than one meaning. Pit can mean "hard seed" or "hole." Read this sentence.

Junk and garbage can be used to fill a pit.

You can find out the meaning of pit in this sentence. Look at the rest of the sentence for clues. The word fill gives you a clue. In this sentence, pit means "hole."

Ask yourself which meaning makes sense. Then, try each meaning in place of the word.

Read each sentence below. Then circle the correct meaning of the word in dark print.

1. People have **set** aside land for plants and animals.

   a. goes down   **c.** matched pair

   b. put

2. The **plants** give food to snails and fish.

   a. puts into ground   **c.** things that grow in the earth

   b. places

3. **Spread** the compost all around your garden.

   a. put over   **c.** butter or jam

   b. tell

4. Drive your car to town and **park** it.

   a. place to play   **c.** place with lots of trees

   b. leave a car in place

Words That Were New to You

Choose words from the story that were new to you. Use a dictionary to check the meanings. Add the words and their meanings to your word list on page 128.

REREADING

Summary

Sometimes you need to go over what you have read. One way is to retell it in your own words. A short retelling of a story is a summary. A summary should tell only the most important ideas. Read this paragraph.

> Things that people throw away are either junk or garbage. Junk and garbage can cause pollution. Some junk and garbage will rot, but some will not.

Now read this summary of the most important idea.

> Some things people throw away will rot.

Read this paragraph from the story. Circle the sentence that gives the best summary.

1. Noise is also a kind of pollution. Very loud noise can make people sick. Noise can hurt people's ears and spoil their hearing.

    a. Noise is very loud.

    b. Loud noise can be bad for people.

    c. It is hard to hear when there is too much noise.

Reread "Pollution," Part 2. How would you retell the important parts? Circle the sentence that gives the best summary of the story.

2. a. Plants and animals need each other to stay alive.

    b. People can hurt the environment, but they can also find ways to save it.

    c. Getting rid of garbage is a very big problem.

Fact and Opinion

A fact is an idea that is true. You can prove it. An opinion is an idea that tells how someone feels or thinks. Write two facts to go with each opinion below. Use page 100 of the story to help you.

1. Opinion: I believe that people should recycle their plastic bottles.

   Facts: _____

   _____

   _____

2. Opinion: I think loud noise should not be allowed.

   Facts: _____

   _____

   _____

STUDY SKILLS

Follow Directions

When you want to learn how to do something, you follow directions. Sometimes directions are written. These ideas can help you follow written directions.

   ▶ First, read all the directions.

   ▶ Look up any words you do not understand.

   ▶ Don't start until you know what to do.

   ▶ Pay special attention to action words. They tell you what to do and what not to do.

   ▶ Be sure you know what to do first, second, next, and last.

Look at the directions on page 108. Then answer the questions.

107

Make Your Own Compost Heap

1. Dig a hole in the ground. Don't make it too deep.

2. Fill the hole with food scraps, leaves, and other things that will rot.

3. Cover the heap with some dirt.

4. Put water on the heap to help it rot.

---

1. What is the first thing you do to make compost?

_____

2. What do you do after you dig the hole?

_____

3. What are the last two things you do?

_____

Check Yourself

Write directions to a place. Give them to a friend.

THINK and WRITE

Use what you have learned to complete one of these activities.

1. Keep track of everything you throw out in one day. What could you use again? Write about it.

2. Make a poster to tell about recycling. List reasons why it is good to recycle. Put the recycle sign on your poster.

3. Brainstorm with your friends. Make a list of ways to recycle books that you don't want anymore.

GETTING READY TO READ

The next story you will read is "And Still the Turtle Watched." It tells how a quiet spot near a river changes over time. What do you think happens to make it change?

What Do You Think You Will Learn?

Look through "And Still the Turtle Watched," Part 1, on pages 110–112. Look at the pictures. Think about the name of the story. What do you think the turtle will see? Write your ideas on the lines below.

_____

_____

_____

_____

_____

_____

And Still the Turtle Watched

PART 1

Long ago when the eagles still built their nests on the cliffs by the river, an old man and his grandson stood beside a large rock.

The rock stood all by itself on the bluff at the bend in the river where the bright water flowed to the bitter sea.

"Here at our summer lodge," the old man said, "I will carve the turtle. He will be the eyes of Manitou the All-Father to watch the Delaware people and he will be our voice to speak to Manitou. In summer you will bring your children to the rock to greet the turtle and they will bring their children. And Manitou will bless our land with plenty, our people with straight bodies and strong arms, and peace shall reign beside our fires."

And so he shaped the stone. And then the turtle watched.

He watched the green of summer turn to the gold of autumn.

He watched the gold of autumn become the white of winter.

He watched the white of winter give birth to the flowers of springtime.

Then summer came again. The turtle was happiest in summer, for then the children came. And then their children, and then their children's children's children.

Year followed year. The Great Bear chased the Little Bear around and around the northern sky. As time wore on, fewer and fewer children came to greet the turtle. Have I watched badly? he thought. Does Manitou no longer hear me?

The rains washed him, the winds blew him, countless snows chilled him, blowing dust rubbed him. Now it took a sharp and knowing eye to see the turtle.

Then one day strangers came. They did not greet the turtle. They did not speak to Manitou. Their axes chopped and killed the forest. Their shouting drowned the lark's bright music. The turtle watched, but did not understand.

He watched as stranger followed stranger followed stranger.

He watched white water turn to brown. He felt the air grow heavy. He heard strange growling noises still the song of birds.

At night new lights glowed near the ground. They dimmed the stars of Manitou.

When you read Part 2 of this story, you will find out what happens to the turtle.

AFTER READING

What Did You Learn?

You have read the first part of "And Still the Turtle Watched." Now look back at what you wrote on page 109. Were you surprised by the changes that the turtle saw? What surprised you the most? Write your answers on the lines below.

_____

_____

_____

Check Your Understanding

Darken the circle next to the word or words that best complete each sentence.

1. The old man carved a _____ out of large rock beside the river.

   Ⓐ fox   Ⓒ turtle

   Ⓑ tree   Ⓓ rabbit

2. The old man carved the turtle to be the eyes of _____.

   Ⓐ Manitou   Ⓒ the summer lodge

   Ⓑ springtime   Ⓓ children

3. The _____ chopped and killed the forest.

   Ⓐ Great Bear   Ⓒ All-Father

   Ⓑ Manitou   Ⓓ strangers

4. The river turned _____ and the songs of the birds were silent.

   Ⓐ white   Ⓒ clear

   Ⓑ brown   Ⓓ blue

Vocabulary — Context Clues

Sometimes a writer uses a word that is new to you. Other words and sentences can give you clues about the meaning of the new word. Read this sentence.

> The rains washed him, the winds blew him, countless snows chilled him.

Other words in this sentence are clues to the meaning of the word chilled. Washed, blew, and snows are all good clue words. Washed tells what the rains did. Blew tells what the winds did. Snows tells that is was cold. You can figure out that chilled means "made cold."

Read these sentences. Use other words to figure out each word in dark print. Then circle the correct meaning.

1. Then one day strangers came. Their shouting **drowned** the lark's bright music.

   a. kept out a sound   **c.** helped make better

   b. hurt on purpose

2. "I will **carve** the turtle to be the eyes of the All-Father," the old man said. And so he shaped the stone.

   a. cut out   **c.** pray

   b. move

3. Long ago, an old man and his grandson stood beside a large rock near a cliff. The rock stood all by itself on the **bluff** near the river.

   a. to fool   **c.** a steep drop

   b. frank and open

Words That Were New to You

Choose words from the story that were new to you. Use a dictionary to check the meanings. Add the words and their meanings to your word list on page 128.

REREADING

Sequence

Knowing the order that things happen in a story helps you understand the story. This order is called sequence. Sometimes writers use clues to help you. Look for clue words such as now, long ago, then, and finally.

Read the following sentences. The words in dark print give clues about the sequence.

> **Long ago** there was a white river. **Years** passed. **Then** one day strangers came. They chopped down trees. The birds stopped singing.

The words in dark print are clues to the order that things happened.

Reread "And Still the Turtle Watched," Part 1, to look for story order. Then, put these sentences in the right order. Write 1, 2, or 3 before each sentence to show the order.

1. _____ The man said he would carve a turtle.

   _____ Long ago a man and a boy stood by a big rock.

   _____ Then the man shaped the stone.

2. _____ At last, the children came and made the turtle happy.

   _____ Summer, autumn, and winter went by.

   _____ Then summer came again.

3. _____ The strangers cut down trees.

   _____ Then one day some strangers came.

   _____ For years rains washed the turtle, and the winds blew him.

Summary

A summary is a way to retell a story in your own words. A summary tells only the most important ideas. Circle the summary that you would use to tell about "And Still the Turtle Watched," Part 1.

1. This story tells about an old Indian man who lived long ago near a river.

2. A long time ago an old Indian man carved a rock turtle. This turtle watched over the Delaware people. Then one day some strangers came and chopped down the forest where the turtle lived. Years passed. The turtle watched as the people ruined the earth.

STUDY SKILLS

Encyclopedia — Cross Reference

An encyclopedia has facts about people, places, and things. You can use an encyclopedia to find out more about something. To look up Recycling, you would look under R. But the R volume might not have all you need. Look at this entry.

> that is why recycling is so important to everyone living on planet Earth.
>
> PETER MOSS
>
> See also ENVIRONMENT; GLASS; INDUSTRY; PAPER; PLASTIC; POLLUTION.

At the end of Recycling, you will find a list of other places in the encyclopedia to find more information about recycling. This page tells you to look under Environment for more information. This list is called a cross reference.

Use what you know about the encyclopedia to answer these questions. Write the letter of the volume you would look for on the line.

_____ **1.** Where would you look next if you found this cross reference in the encyclopedia?

   Littering: See Pollution.

_____ **2.** Where would you look next if you found this cross reference in the encyclopedia?

   Compost: See Fertilizer.

_____ **3.** Where would you look next if you found this cross reference in the encyclopedia?

   Sewage: See Wastewater.

Check Yourself

Look up one of the cross references above in the encyclopedia. Did you find more information?

THINK and WRITE

Use what you have learned to complete one of these activities.

1. Imagine that the old man who carved the turtle was your grandfather. Tell what you saw and felt when you watched him shape the big rock.

2. Think of a beautiful place you enjoy visiting—a park, a beach, or maybe a mountain. Write a story about what could happen if people stopped caring for that place.

3. Find out about the Delaware Indians. Use an encyclopedia to help you. Look for cross references that might help you. Write a summary about what you find.

GETTING READY TO READ

In the first part of "And Still the Turtle Watched," you read about a turtle carved out of a rock. What happened to the river where the turtle watched? Why did fewer and fewer children come to greet the turtle?

What Do You Think You Will Learn?

Look through "And Still the Turtle Watched," Part 2, on pages 119–122. What do you think will happen to the turtle now? Write your ideas below.

_____

_____

_____

_____

_____

_____

And Still the Turtle Watched

PART 2

The little turtle grew very sad. Why do I watch? he thought. Why do I speak to Manitou when Manitou no longer hears me? The air is dark and dirty. The stars are dim. The noises hurt my ears. My children have not come for many times many moons.

In the night the turtle wept.

One day some boys came near the rock. They stopped and pointed. The turtle's heart beat faster. "They've come to see me," he murmured to himself. "My children have returned. Thank you, Manitou."

He watched them as they capered around him. Black boxes on their shoulders blared loud noise that hurt the turtle's ears. They pointed shiny round things at him.

The turtle heard a hiss. He saw a shining arc of color leap toward him. He felt cool wetness on his eyes. He could no longer see. He could no longer watch for Manitou. Deep in his darkness he felt the cracking of his heart.

No one watched for Manitou as days, months, and years passed, and the turtle stood in darkness. Then one day a man came. He knew that the Delaware people had once summered here. He hoped to find something they had left behind, but searched all day and found nothing. He was tired. He was going home.

Suddenly he saw the rock standing all by itself on the bluff at the bend in the river where the bright water flows to the bitter sea.

Something about the rock called to him as it stood forlorn and covered with graffiti. He was a man who saw beneath what first appeared. He had a sharp and knowing eye, he had a wise and loving heart, he knew the ways of Manitou.

The turtle did not know the man was there. The paint had blinded his eyes. The paint had stopped up his ears. Then he felt a finger on his head. It stroked back along his carapace and he shivered deep inside.

The man came back with workmen. They pried the rock out of the ground and hoisted it up on a truck. The little turtle was very frightened. He did not know what was happening.

The truck swayed and bumped along for a long long time. Then the rock was hoisted off the truck. Hands patted and rubbed the turtle. He felt sharp-smelling wetness pour over his head and his eyes started to clear and his ears to hear as the paint was scrubbed away.

No longer is he watching by the river. He is indoors at the botanical garden where the children come to see him. And they will bring their children, and their children's children's children. And he will speak of them to Manitou.

From *And Still The Turtle Watched,* by Sheila MacGill-Calahan

The turtle you just read about is in the New York Botanical Garden. If you live in New York City or plan to visit, you can see it there.

AFTER READING

What Did You Learn?

You have read Part 2 of "And Still the Turtle Watched" for the first time. Now look back at what you wrote on page 118. Were you surprised by what happened to the turtle at the end? Why or why not? Write your answers below.

_____

_____

_____

Check Your Understanding

Darken the circle next to the word or words that best complete each sentence.

1. When the children stopped visiting, the turtle believed that _____ no longer heard him.

   Ⓐ the old man   Ⓒ Great Bear

   Ⓑ Delaware   Ⓓ Manitou

2. Some loud boys sprayed _____ on the turtle.

   Ⓐ paint   Ⓒ water

   Ⓑ dirt   Ⓓ grass

3. The turtle was covered with _____.

   Ⓐ water   Ⓒ graffiti

   Ⓑ leaves   Ⓓ snow

4. The wise man took the turtle indoors to the botanical _____.

   Ⓐ stream   Ⓒ black box

   Ⓑ garden   Ⓓ grass

Vocabulary — Homophones

Homophones are words that sound the same but have different spellings and meanings. Beat and beet are homophones. Beat means "to pound." Beet is a kind of vegetable. You can use the spelling and other words in a sentence to help you figure out the meaning of a homophone.

Read this sentence. Which homophone is correct?

The turtle's heart (beat   beet) faster.

The words heart and faster are clues. You know that a heart can pound. You know it can pound faster and faster. So the correct homophone is beat.

Read each sentence below. You might need to look up the homophones in dark print in your dictionary first. Circle the correct homophone. Then, circle its meaning.

1. The river flowed out to the **(see   sea)**.

   a. large body   **b.** to look at
       of water

2. The turtle could not see **(threw   through)** the paint.

   a. from one side to   **b.** tossed
       the other

3. The man **(new   knew)** the ways of Manitou.

   a. understood   **b.** never used before

4. The old man said, "Peace will **(reign   rain)** over the land."

   a. rule   **b.** falling water

Words That Were New to You

Choose words from the story that were new to you. Use a dictionary to check the meanings. Add the words and their meanings to your word list on page 128.

REREADING

Drawing Conclusions

Writers don't always tell you everything. Some story ideas you have to figure out. You can use story clues and what you already know to help you. This is called drawing conclusions. Read these story clues about what the boys did to the turtle.

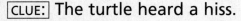

CLUE: The turtle heard a hiss.

CLUE: He saw a shining arc of color leap toward him.

CLUE: He felt cool wetness on his eyes.

The writer doesn't tell you that the boys sprayed paint. You can figure this out by using the story clues.

Reread "And Still the Turtle Watched," Part 2. Use the story clues and what you know to help you complete each sentence. Circle the best answer. Then, write two story clues that helped you.

1. After the boys sprayed paint at him, the turtle was
   _____. (page 120)

   a. very happy   **c.** very sad

   b. very angry

   CLUE: _____

   CLUE: _____

2. Now that the turtle can see and hear, he is _____.
   (page 122)

   a. very happy   **c.** not very happy

   b. lonely

   CLUE: _____

   CLUE: _____

Sequence

The order that things happen in a story is called
sequence. Read each sentence. Then, tell two things that
happened next.

1. The man came back with workmen.

   What happened next?

   Next: _____

   Then: _____

2. The workers scrubbed the paint off the rock turtle.

   What happened next?

   Next: _____

   Then: _____

STUDY SKILLS

Using Library Resources

The library has many ways to help you find the
information and books you need. One way is to use the
card catalog or computer catalog. A catalog has three
kinds of cards or files. They are all listed in alphabetical
order.

There are book, author, and topic cards or files.

► You can look up the name of a book.
   Delaware Tales would be listed under D.

► You can look up the name of an author.
   Virginia Hamilton would be listed under H.

► You can look up a topic.
   Delaware Indians would be listed under D.

Use what you know about the library to answer each question. Circle the correct answer.

1. Where would you look to find a book written by Harold Courlander?

   a. author card or file under C

   b. author card or file under H

2. Where would you find the book *Stone Fox*?

   a. topic card or file under S

   b. book card or file under S

3. Where would you find a book about pollution?

   a. topic card or file under P

   b. book card or file under P

Check Yourself

Pick one of the questions. Go to the library. Use the catalog to find the book. Which kind of card or file did you use?

Use what you have learned to complete one of these activities.

1. Imagine that you can visit the garden where the turtle now lives. Write in your journal about how the turtle looks. Tell how you feel when you see the turtle.

2. The garden is having a contest to name the turtle. What name would you give the turtle? Explain your answer.

3. What would it be like to be a rock sitting on the edge of a river? Write a poem about it.

MY WORD LIST